STO

Bells for a
Chinese Donkey

Bells for a

Chinese Donkey

WRITTEN AND ILLUSTRATED BY

ELEANOR FRANCES LATTIMORE

WILLIAM MORROW & COMPANY

NEW YORK · 1951

Second Printing, January, 1952

CHAPTERS

Bells for a
Chinese Donkey

Chapter One

KWEI-LI AND HER BROTHER SHAN

LITTLE Kwei-li was the youngest one in her family, but that did not mean she was an unimportant person. The world spread around her from the blue sea to the far-off mountains, and the center of this world was little Kwei-li. Her mother and father loved her and did not scold her often. Her older brother was good to her

and hardly ever teased her.   Though the family
was poor, that did not trouble Kwei-li, who was
no richer and no poorer than any of her friends.

When Kwei-li opened her eyes in the morning, the first thing she saw was a paper bird out-
lined against the paper-paned window.   The
bird had been given to her by her brother Shan,
who had bought it at a fair in the nearest market
town.   It was as yellow as a canary, with a tail
as long as a pheasant's, but the whistle inside
that made it sing had somehow been broken.

Kwei-li loved the paper bird, even though it
had no whistle.   It perched upon a bamboo rod
just like a living bird.   The morning sun shone
on it; the slightest breeze made it sway.

"It is only a paper toy," said Shan.

"No, it's a bird," said Kwei-li.

The village where Kwei-li lived was on the
seacoast of China.   Her home was small, just

two rooms within a walled courtyard, but it was large enough for the family of four: her father, her mother, her brother Shan, and Kwei-li herself.

In winter, when the wind swept across the northern plains or blew even more fiercely from across the sea, Kwei-li's mother was glad that the house was not larger, for one stove could keep her family snug and warm. And as for the summer, who needed a large house then? Neither of the children ever stayed indoors in warm weather. They both had big straw hats to shield their heads from the sun, and as soon as they had eaten their breakfast they put on their big straw hats.

Kwei-li was five years old. When she grew bigger she would learn how to sweep the floors and polish the best teakettle. She would wash the rice bowls with goldfish painted on them, and help her mother fold the quilts on the straw-matted bed. Now she was too young to help her mother, for her hands were too small to be useful in the house. But her feet, in red cloth shoes, were not too small to carry her up and down the village street or out to the fields. Millet grew in the fields, with black beans planted between the rows, and beyond the fields was the sea. Closer to the village were vegetable patches, one of which belonged to Kwei-li's family.

Shan was ten years old, old enough to help his father, who was a farmer and a fisherman as well. Shan longed to go out at sunrise with the fishing fleet to help his father and the other men manage their great net. The net was heavy when they lowered it in the sea, but heavier still when they dragged it to shore. Many fish were caught in it, big ones and small ones.

"Let me go out in your boat with you!" Shan begged his father.

But his father said, "The tides change, and the sea is rough. It is better for small boys like you to stay on the shore. When you are older and stronger you can be a fisherman, but now you can help me by learning to be a farmer."

So Shan hoed the weeds in the vegetable garden while he dreamed of going out with the fishing fleet. And Kwei-li, free to do as she pleased, kept him company as she hunted for singing crickets among the growing plants. Shan was tall and serious, and Kwei-li was small and cheerful, but they looked very much alike in their big straw hats.

One morning in the early summer Shan and Kwei-li started out right after breakfast toward the vegetable patch. The lazy village watch-dogs lay in the sun, for they knew that strangers hardly ever came this way. At the edge of the village a path dipped down to the lower land where the gardens lay. Shan, shouldering his hoe, followed the path, and Kwei-li, holding a small box, pattered after him.

Kwei-li felt very happy. If she caught a cricket she would put it in the box and listen to it sing. But Shan's eyes gazed past the fields to the sea, where the fishing boats were distant specks. He was sure that he could be a good fisherman if his father would only let him try. He would sell his share of fish in the market town. Then, thought Shan, our family would be rich.

Shan decided that if he were rich he would buy a big boat with a sail. He would wear a silk jacket and eat sesame-seed candy. Ay-ah, he thought, it is good to be rich!

Suddenly there came a sound of jingling

bells. Shan, who had just begun to hoe, straightened up to listen.

"The dogs are barking," said Kwei-li, moving closer to Shan. Yes, the village dogs were barking at the sound of bells.

The path that led through the fields was too narrow for a cart but, since the dogs were barking, strangers must be coming. The jingling bells grew louder as a donkey appeared.

"It is only a donkey," said Shan. But it was not only a donkey.

There were one, two, three donkeys, one behind the other, all trotting briskly down the path from the village. Each donkey had a rider, and the riders all were strangers. Shan and Kwei-li stared at them from under their straw hats. Two of the riders were grown people, a man and a woman, but it was the third rider that Kwei-li watched. She was a little girl not much bigger than Kwei-li, and she rode on the donkey with the jingling bells.

The little girl was so prettily dressed and the donkey looked so gay that Kwei-li smiled, forgetting to be shy of a stranger. The little girl smiled back. In a moment she had passed by, and the donkey bells jingled fainter and fainter in the distance.

Shan drew a deep sigh and went back to his work. "Those were rich people," he said to Kwei-li. "They must live beyond the rocky point where the summer houses are."

Kwei-li nodded, listening to the donkey bells.

Her father, who often traveled far in his boat, had told them about the fine homes where people from the city came to spend the summer months. Kwei-li had never seen their houses and gardens. She didn't know those people, and they didn't know her.

But now, as she started to hunt for a cricket, she thought of the little girl who had ridden by on her donkey. "It must be good to be rich like that little girl," she said to Shan. "It must be good to be rich and ride on a beautiful donkey."

Chapter Two

A SURPRISE FOR KWEI-LI

THE village that Kwei-li lived in was called Locust Village because of the locusts that sang in the pine trees in the village square. There were only three pine trees, but there were many locusts, and their humming tune sounded all through the summer months.

One morning when Kwei-li woke up she heard the locusts, but she didn't hear her father's voice or her brother's voice. The house seemed very quiet. She saw only her mother and the paper bird on its bamboo perch. Kwei-li sat up straight in bed. "Where has Shan gone?" she asked. She was used to her father's leaving early, but she missed Shan.

"Shan left the house with your father before the sun rose," said her mother. "They have gone to the market town."

"Have they gone to a fair?" asked Kwei-li.

Her mother nodded. "They have gone to buy something," she said. "The men have had good luck this week; they have caught many fish. Your father will sell fish at the market and he will bring something back."

Maybe another paper bird, with a whistle, thought Kwei-li.

Then Kwei-li wanted to know why her father hadn't taken her. She had never been to the market town in all her life.

"Your feet could not walk so far," her mother told her.

"I have my shoes," said Kwei-li. "New ones." She looked at them proudly.

"You would wear holes in your new shoes if you walked so far," said her mother.

Kwei-li did not want to wear holes in her new shoes. They were red, with a line of green binding around the edges. Her mother had made her these new shoes when her old ones began to wear out, and it had taken her a long time to make all the tiny stitches. First she had cut the pattern, just the right size for Kwei-li's feet. Next she had cut the bright red cloth the same shape as the pattern. But the soles of the shoes, made of layers of white cloth, were what took the longest time to sew. They were stitched together with hundreds of stitches to make them firm and strong.

Kwei-li looked at her old shoes. They were red, too, but the color had faded and there were holes in the toes. "I am going to wear my new shoes all the time," she told her mother.

"Take care of your new shoes," said her mother, smiling.

While Kwei-li ate her breakfast of yellow corn meal, she thought about Shan's shoes and hoped he wouldn't wear holes in them. | It was many miles to the market town and as many miles back—five miles or ten, she wasn't sure which.

Shan and her father would not return till nightfall, so there was a whole day to wait until they came back. There was a whole day in which to wonder what they would bring home with them.

"Do you know?" Kwei-li asked her mother.

"Yes.   But it is a surprise."

Kwei-li's mother had work to do, cleaning the house and mending clothes, and she did not think that Kwei-li was old enough to help her. "Run and play," she said, "but do not go far."

Kwei-li promised her mother not to go beyond the village.

Shan's hoe leaned against the courtyard wall. There was no one to use it today, for Shan was not here.   But the courtyard was not as deserted as it seemed, because four brown hens were cackling in the straw-filled shed.   One of them had just laid an egg.   Kwei-li found it.   She carried it to her mother before going out to play.

The gate that led to the street was closed, but

Kwei-li opened it and went out into the village to see what was happening there. The first person she saw was a little girl named Bluebell, who was three years older than Kwei-li and always busy. Bluebell was minding her little brother, and he was trying to run away from her. When he reached the path that led to the fields, Bluebell caught him and carried him, laughing and kicking, back to his own home.

Bluebell was tired and out of breath when Kwei-li came up to her. "You are very lucky," she said to Kwei-li. "You do not have to mind your brother. Your brother looks after *you.*"

"My brother has gone to the market today," announced Kwei-li.

Bluebell sat down on her doorstep, holding her wiggling brother beside her. Her eyes were bright and curious. "Tell me about it," she said. "What did he go to the market for? And what will he bring back?"

Kwei-li could not tell her. That was to be a surprise. "But I think he will bring me back some kind of toy," she said. "Or maybe he will bring me a beautiful paper bird."

"You have one," Bluebell pointed out.

"But it does not sing," said Kwei-li.

There was room for two birds side by side on the bamboo perch. And two birds would be better than one, Kwei-li thought. When Blue-bell's brother struggled free and darted down the street again, Kwei-li went on her way to see what other friends she could find.

In the village square she saw two boys, friends of Shan's, who were too busy to look up from their game of checkers. Their board was made of lines drawn in the dust, and their men were pebbles.

"Shan has gone to the market town," Kwei-li said to them.

"He told us," said the boy named Li, without looking up.

"Did he tell you what he was going to buy?" asked Kwei-li.

"He was not going to buy anything," said the boy named Lan jokingly. "It's your turn," he said to Li, studying the checkers game.

Kwei-li walked on, feeling a little anxious. Surely Shan would bring something back! Her mother had said so. It might not be a paper bird, but it would be something nice— something to look at or something to play with. Kwei-li wished she knew.

In the very last house of the village there lived an old lady, who often sat in her doorway sewing when the sun was not too hot. She was older than anyone else in the village and she was called Great-grandmother. Kwei-li hurried to the old lady's house in her new red shoes.

Great-grandmother sat in the sun, for it was not too hot today. She smiled when she saw Kwei-li. "What pretty new shoes," she said.

"I could not go to the market town in these new shoes," said Kwei-li. "But Shan went with my father. They will bring something back."

Great-grandmother knew all about the trip to the market. "Your mother told me about the trip," she said to Kwei-li. "You will have another mouth to feed—a big, big mouth."

Kwei-li was so astonished that her own mouth opened wide. Another mouth to feed meant another person. Was her father going to bring home a visitor—a stranger? "Who is coming home with my father and Shan, Great-grandmother?" she asked.

But Great-grandmother would not tell her. It was to be a surprise. All she would say was that there would be company that night. As Kwei-li started home, she said, "Tell your hens to make room."

Kwei-li walked home, more puzzled than ever. All day she wondered about the company and, when evening came with no Shan, and no father, she began to feel worried. Her mother, wondering if something had happened, began to look worried too. Maybe they had not been able to buy what they wanted.

Kwei-li was falling asleep when voices sounded in the courtyard. The hens were cackling—or *were* they cackling? What was all that noise? It sounded like a donkey braying. It *was* a donkey! There were Shan, her father, and the company—a donkey they had bought at the market!

Kwei-li was wide-awake in a moment. "Were you surprised?" asked Shan.

Kwei-li nodded, too glad to speak. She liked the surprise. She borrowed some hay from the hens and offered it to the visitor, who she hoped would stay in her family for a long, long time.

Chapter Three

KWEI-LI AND SHAN GO RIDING

THERE were other donkeys in Locust Village besides the new donkey that Shan and Kwei-li's father had bought at the fair. There were several that helped the farmers in the spring and fall plowing, and there was one that turned the grindstone that ground millet into meal.

33

But none of these donkeys was as handsome as theirs, thought Shan and Kwei-li, admiring the newcomer. His coat was smooth and gray, with a black stripe down his back and another black stripe across his shoulders.

The donkey had to have a name.

Shan wanted to call him Grayback because of his smooth gray coat. "I will call him Grayback," said Shan.

But Kwei-li wanted to call him Longlegs, because of his long legs. "I am going to call our donkey Longlegs," she said to Shan.

Their father said, "You children may call him anything you choose, but he is a donkey and his name is Donkey."

Shan and Kwei-li nodded gravely. There was no denying that. They decided to call their donkey by his true name, Donkey.

The children's mother sighed when, the very

next morning, Shan and Kwei-li declared that
they wanted to go for a ride. She herself had
never learned to ride a donkey and preferred
to walk on the firm ground. Besides, as she
pointed out, this donkey had been bought for
work. He could carry grain in saddlebags
slung across his back. He could be taught to
pull the plow or turn the grindstone. There
were a great many uses for the long-legged,
gray-backed donkey. C410987 CO. SCHOOLS

But Shan and Kwei-li thought that a donkey
was meant for pleasure. They could hardly
wait to get on Donkey's back and go trotting
through the village. Hadn't Shan ridden him
home safely? And hadn't Kwei-li seen a little
girl like herself on a donkey?

They were not at all afraid. So they turned
to their father, begging him to let them go for
a ride.

"May we ride through the fields?" asked Kwei-li.

"May we ride to the shore?" asked Shan.

"You must learn how to stay on the donkey's back first," said their father.

Shan and Kwei-li watched their father put a saddle on Donkey. It was a cloth saddle, blue with red borders. They watched him slip the bit between Donkey's teeth and toss the bridle over his head. Donkey shifted his hoofs impatiently.

"He wants to start," said Kwei-li.

Her father tightened the band that held the saddle in place, before he lifted the children to Donkey's back—first Shan, then Kwei-li. "Hold tight to the reins," he told Shan. "Hold tight to Shan," he told Kwei-li. "Now walk, but do not run," he told the donkey.

Donkey's long ears pointed toward the gateway. He wanted to go through the gate and he wanted to run. When Father's hand let go of the bridle, Donkey leapt over the door-sill.

"Wait," called Father. "Wait!" cried Mother. But Donkey did not wait.

Shan had ridden Donkey home from the market town, but that was at the end of the day, and perhaps Donkey had been tired. Now, after a night's rest and plenty of hay, he felt very frisky. He galloped down the street, kicking up dust clouds as he ran. Shan held tight to the reins, but he could not stay on the saddle. Up and down he bounced, while Kwei-li bounced behind him.

"Ay-ah," cried all the village children, running to their doorways. "Look at Shan and Kwei-li riding on their donkey!"

Kwei-li tried to smile between the bounces.

She was riding on a donkey just like the rich little girl, but she felt very queer. She felt as though she were flying. She shut her eyes, and her short arms clasped Shan tightly.

Chickens scattered to right and left before the galloping donkey. Two small boys, Li and Lan, jumped up and down. "Your donkey is running away!" they cried. "Make your donkey stop!" But neither Shan nor Kwei-li knew how to make Donkey stop.

There were many people gathered in the village square, where women were drying jellyfish in the sun. Jellyfish were good to eat when dried just right, and Great-grandmother was telling the others what to do. Nobody expected to see a runaway donkey with two children clinging wildly to its back. And the donkey surely never expected to see all the jellyfish. Suddenly it stopped short.

"Ay-ah!" cried all the women.

The well that provided water for everyone in the village was in the very center of the square; and there was Shan, his grip loosened by the sudden stop, flying over Donkey's head, just missing the well!

At the same moment poor Kwei-li went sailing over Donkey's back before anyone could catch her. She landed, plop, in the middle of a large jellyfish.

"Ay-ah!" cried all the women. "What a wicked donkey!"

Kwei-li hardly knew what had happened to her, but she heard what the women said and she felt the jellyfish. She picked herself up hastily and looked around her, wondering whether to laugh or to cry.

The other village children, who had no donkey, began to laugh, and that made Kwei-li feel like crying. But Shan was not crying. He had picked himself up and was holding Donkey firmly by the bridle.

Kwei-li smiled through her tears. She went over to Donkey, who was meekly standing still, hanging his head. "This is not a wicked donkey. This is *our* donkey," she said. "Our donkey was frightened by the wicked jellyfish."

Everyone was laughing now; and when Kwei-li's father came running into the square to catch the runaway donkey, he found a gentle, quiet beast, surrounded by smiling faces. How quickly children learn how to manage animals, he thought.

It really did seem as though Donkey knew that he belonged to Kwei-li and Shan, for after that day they never had any trouble with him at all. He learned to stop when they told him to stop, and to trot if they told him to trot. But they never rode him into the square again when there were jellyfish drying.

They rode him through the fields, however, and they rode him to the shore. Even their mother grew used to the sight of Shan and Kwei-li on Donkey. Shan always sat in front, holding the reins with both hands, and Kwei-li, with pigtails flying, rode gaily behind him.

Chapter Four

HOW KWEI-LI LOST A SHOE

THE beach below Locust Village was shaped like a half moon. It curved between two points of rocks. Beyond the farther point lived the city people who came to spend the summer months at the seashore. Shan, with some other boys, had explored the far-off rocks, but Kwei-li knew only the shore that was nearest to her home. The rocks below the village were not such big ones, and they did not jut out quite so far into the sea.

Though Shan was not allowed to go out with the fishing fleet, he could wade in the water with a small net on a stick. When the tide was low, he often found fish in shallow pools—little fish that he could scoop up into his net.

One morning Shan and Kwei-li rode down to the beach on Donkey. The tide was out, and a sand bar stretched across the smooth bay. Shan was planning to fish, so he had brought his net with him, holding it carefully as he rode.

Kwei-li never caught fish, but sometimes she found seaweed that was curly like lettuce and good to eat. More often she found sea shells, which she took home to play with. She hoped she could find some sea shells today.

The only shells that Kwei-li collected were the pretty ones. They had to be double shells, and she liked the pink ones best. She arranged them in families, with a father and mother, and a whole row of small shells for the children.

When Kwei-li and Shan reached the beach they slid off their donkey, who had stopped exactly when they told him to. There was nothing on the beach but some fishing boats pulled up above the high-tide line. There was nothing at all to tie Donkey to, which was something the children had not thought about.

"You had better stay with him and hold the bridle," said Shan.

Kwei-li held the bridle, but her face grew sad, for she wanted to walk along the beach and look for shells. She could not look for shells and lead the donkey at the same time. If she let go of the bridle, he might stray away.

"Let's take turns," said Kwei-li. "I will stay with Donkey now. But then, in a little while, you must hold the bridle."

Shan did not answer. He was taking off his shoes and rolling his trousers up above his knees.

All Kwei-li wanted to do was hunt for shells. What good were shells, Shan thought. He was here to work, for fishing was work, while gathering shells was only play. So Shan waded out into the shallow water without glancing back at his little sister. He would not be gone long and, when he came back, he would have some small fish shining in his net.

Kwei-li waited. She watched her brother wading out to the long sand bar. Waves rippled over it, for the tide was coming in. Shan's net dipped, and Kwei-li wondered if he had caught a fish.

But Shan did not catch that fish. It slipped away. Perhaps he would have better luck near the rocks, he thought. The incoming tide had not reached the pools between the rocks, which were partly on the land and partly in the sea.

Shan disappeared behind a rock, and Kwei-li could not even see the peak of his straw hat. Donkey stamped his hoofs, and Kwei-li felt impatient, for she did not like to be left so long holding the bridle. Five minutes seemed like half an hour; ten minutes seemed like an hour.

"Shan! Shan!" Kwei-li called. But Shan did not hear her. He was much too busy. He had almost caught a jellyfish, and he might yet get one.

"Come, Donkey," said Kwei-li. "We will go and find Shan." But she could not climb on Donkey's back all by herself, and she did not want to lead him out into the water, because she

had on her new red shoes. Her mother had
told her to take care of them, and Kwei-li didn't
want to get them wet or to take them off.

Things got lost if you left them on the beach,
for the tide came up, and up, and carried them
away. No! She decided to leave her shoes on
and climb over the dry rocks, leading Donkey.

Kwei-li could scramble over rocks as nimbly
as a crab, and the sure-footed donkey knew how
to climb, too. Kwei-li had no trouble leading
him up onto the nearest rock—but there Donkey stopped and refused to go farther.

"Come, Donkey," said Kwei-li, tugging at
the bridle. What was the matter with her gentle donkey? The trouble was that he didn't
want to jump across to the next rock, which was
separated from the first by a narrow crack.

Kwei-li let go of Donkey and jumped across
the crack. "Come," she said.

But Donkey would not follow. He stood still, as though he were a part of the rock.

"Shan! Shan!" Kwei-li called again, but still Shan did not answer.

Kwei-li scrambled up to the top of the second rock. It was higher than the first, and she could see Shan now. He was wading in a pool beside one of the farther rocks. If she went closer, she might be able to make him hear her.

Meanwhile, Shan had just caught two beautiful fish, and he wanted to take them home to his mother right away. He splashed back, around the rocks, toward the beach. "Look, Kwei-li!" he called, holding his net high.

But where was Kwei-li? She was nowhere in sight. There was only the gray donkey, standing braying upon a rock.

Then Shan heard his sister calling, "Shan, Shan, come and find me!"

Her voice came from midway along the rocky point. Shan dropped his net with the fish in it and hurried to find her. There was poor Kwei-li, caught in a deep crack. Her foot had slipped and she had fallen between two great rocks.

Shan knew what to do. He lay down on his stomach and reached down his arms until his hands caught Kwei-li's hands. "Climb, Kwei-li," he said. "Climb, and I will pull you." In a few moments Kwei-li was up out of the crack.

Kwei-li had not cried before, but now she was crying.

"Smile, Kwei-li," said Shan. "What are you crying for?"

"I have lost my shoe," sobbed Kwei-li. "My *new* shoe." Sure enough, one shoe was gone!

Shan peered into the deep crack, and so did Kwei-li, but they could not see the red shoe wedged deeply down. Soon the tide would come in and carry it out to sea. Kwei-li could not stop the tears that rolled down her cheeks.

Shan tried to comfort her. Hadn't he caught two fine fish? And hadn't the donkey stood still, without trying to run away? The fish were there in the net, and Donkey was ready to take them home. After all, Kwei-li's mother could make her another shoe.

When the children reached home safe and sound, their mother was glad to see them, but she was puzzled when they told her about Kwei-li's mishap. "Why didn't you take your shoes off, like Shan?" she asked Kwei-li.

"Because they were so new," said Kwei-li, wiping her eyes.

Her mother understood, so she did not scold Kwei-li. "Never mind," she said. "I will make you another shoe."

"How soon?" asked Kwei-li, smiling once more.

"Very soon," replied her mother. "But right now I am going to cook the fish that Shan caught this morning!"

Chapter Five

HOW KWEI-LI WEEDED THE GARDEN

KWEI-LI'S mother searched through the scraps
of cloth in her workbox. Kwei-li must have
a new shoe as soon as she could make one. She
must have a new shoe exactly like the other.
Here was white cloth to make the sole and red
cloth for the sides. But Kwei-li's mother could

not find any green cloth to bind the edges like the other shoe. There was some blue cloth, however.

"Will this do?" she asked Kwei-li.

Kwei-li shook her head. It must be just like the other.

Her mother thought a moment. She knew that her cousin who lived in the next village had some green cloth. She had made a little green coat for her youngest son, and surely there must be a few scraps left over. She decided to send Shan on an errand to the next village. He could ride there and back on Donkey, and it would not take him long. When he returned he would bring some green cloth for the binding of Kwei-li's shoe.

"It is lucky we have a donkey," said Kwei-li's mother.

It is lucky we have a donkey, thought Kwei-li.   But it was unlucky that she had lost her shoe.   Until the new one could be finished, she had to walk around with one foot in a new shoe and one foot in an old one.   The old shoe was too small for her, and one of her toes pushed through a hole in it.

"Hole-in-the-toe," said Bluebell, laughing at her.

"Hole-in-the-toe," repeated Bluebell's little brother.

"My mother is making me a new shoe," Kwei-li explained.

Bluebell's own shoes were old and faded. She wished that her mother would make her some new ones, but her mother thought that Bluebell should learn to sew herself.   Bluebell thought she was kept too busy minding her brother.

Bluebell felt cross about her shoes, so she

teased Kwei-li. "I saw your brother Shan ride by on the donkey," she said. "The donkey belongs to Shan. It is not yours."

"It is partly mine," said Kwei-li.

"Which part?" asked Bluebell. "The head or the tail?"

Kwei-li did not know how to answer that question, so she walked away from Bluebell toward her own home. "I am busy," she called back over her shoulder. "I haven't time to talk to you any more."

But when she reached the gateway of her courtyard, Kwei-li paused, for she didn't really have any work to do. Her mother would not let her polish the teakettle or do the other household tasks that older girls learned.

An idea suddenly came to her. She could work in the garden! The hoe was too heavy for her, but she could pull up weeds with her hands. Shan had gone on an errand for her, so she in turn could help Shan. He would be glad to find the garden weeded when he returned.

There was no hunting of crickets for Kwei-li today. She had work to do, she told herself. As she hurried down the path to her family's vegetable patch she felt very glad that she had work to do.

Few people were in the fields, since no planting was being done just now. A single farmer was hoeing weeds in a neighboring patch. Farther away two boys, Li and Lan, were raking around some plants.

Li and Lan did not see Kwei-li at first, and the farmer, if he noticed her, paid no attention. Kwei-li stood for a moment at the edge of her garden, trying to remember what each plant was. These feathery green things near her feet were carrot tops; she knew that. Carrots were good to eat when they grew big enough. Donkeys liked carrots, too. Kwei-li pulled up a carrot to see if it were big enough for herself or Donkey to eat.

But the carrot was very small, for it had not been growing long. Kwei-li ate it just the same. It tasted of dirt. The carrots did not need to be weeded yet, she decided. She would leave them alone so that they could grow big.

The plants in the next row were like tiny bushes, and Kwei-li knew what they were too. They were beans. Slender green beans clustered under the heart-shaped leaves. Kwei-li ate a tender bean, but it did not taste good either. The beans would be good to eat when they grew bigger, and when her mother had cooked them with a little oil. Kwei-li saw no weeds among the beans, so she walked on a bit. Surely she could find some plants that needed weeding.

Beyond the beans were onions. Anyone could tell what they were because of the delicious onion smell. The smell made Kwei-li hungry and she thought of hastening home to dinner. But she must find some weeds to pull up first. There were no weeds among the onions, so she walked on.

Here, hidden behind the onions, were some sprawling leaves which did not look like anything that Kwei-li had ever seen before. Weeds, she thought, pulling the green leaves out of the dirt. There were some more a short way off, and over there were still more.

Kwei-li was so busy pulling up weeds that she forgot to feel hungry and to wonder about dinner. But Li and Lan were hungry. They

were shouldering their rakes, ready to start
home, when they spied Kwei-li.

"Kwei-li!" called Li. "What are you do-
ing?"

"Kwei-li!" called Lan. "Shan will be an-
gry!"

Kwei-li, startled, flung down the last weed
she had pulled up. "What is the matter?" she
said. "I am only weeding the garden."

Li and Lan hurried over to where Kwei-li
stood. Their eyes were round with amazement
as they looked at the work she had done.
"Don't you know that those are watermelon
plants?" they said. "You have pulled up all
your father's watermelon plants!"

Kwei-li opened her mouth, but she could not
say a word. So those weedy-looking plants
were watermelon vines! Her father prided
himself on his fine watermelons. But there

were no melons on the vines yet, not a single
one.

"How should I know that they were watermelons?" Kwei-li said at last. "Shan never
told me."

"Shan never told you to weed the garden,"
said Li sternly.

"There are some left," said Kwei-li in a small
voice, pointing.

Yes, there were just three vines left growing
at the end of the row that was farthest from the
village. Those would grow, thought Kwei-li
hopefully. They would grow and grow, for
nobody would pull them up.

Kwei-li would not eat her dinner and, when
her mother asked her why, she told about the
work she had done that morning.

"Ay-ah!" cried her mother in distress. "All
our watermelon plants!"

"Not all, Mother," said Kwei-li. "There are three left."

Kwei-li's mother did not scold her, for Kwei-li was sorry, and fearful of what her father and Shan would say. "We will just hope that those three vines are strong ones," her mother said, "and that the melons will be very big."

When Shan came home with the green cloth he felt very happy, because he had had a good ride to the next village and back. He was not cross about the melons, and neither was Kwei-li's father when he returned home from a good fishing trip. But they agreed that little girls should not try to weed gardens.

"Leave the vegetables alone and let them grow," said Kwei-li's father.

There were only three melon vines left, but they were fine, strong ones. Perhaps the melons on these vines would be extra big!

Chapter Six

THE SILVER BRACELET

KWEI-LI'S father was proud of his vegetable garden. No farmer grew finer vegetables than his. When the beans were ready to pick and it was time to pull up the carrots and turnips, he worked in the garden with Shan instead of going fishing.

"Look!" he said. "The carrots are as red as coral, and these round, young turnips are like pearls."

Shan agreed. But he wished they were real coral and real pearls, for vegetables did not make people rich.

One day when Shan and Kwei-li went into the courtyard they saw their father filling two baskets with vegetables. He was arranging cabbages around the edges of the wide, shallow baskets and putting turnips, carrots, and bunches of onions in the center.

Kwei-li had never seen vegetables looking so pretty. "What are you going to do with them, Father?" she asked.

"I am going to sell them," replied her father. "We have more than enough for ourselves, and they are such beautiful, fresh ones that I ought to get a good price."

Shan was excited. "Are you going to the market?" he asked, hoping that his father would let him go with him.

But his father said there was no need to go as far as the market town. He planned to sell these vegetables to the rich summer visitors.

Shan and Kwei-li watched their father fasten the baskets to a long, bamboo pole with hooks on both ends. He was going to carry the baskets beyond the far rocky point, taking the shortest road through the fields of millet.

Shan wanted to go with his father. Since he had helped to grow the vegetables, it seemed only right to him that he should help sell them. And Kwei-li wanted to go with Shan.

"Let us ride Donkey!" they cried. If they rode on Donkey's back, the road would not seem long.

But their father shook his head. He preferred to walk, he said. He had arranged the vegetables just so, and he did not want them to spill. But if the children wished to come, they could ride Donkey. Shan might fill a small basket of his own and sell vegetables too.

The children were both very happy. While Shan saddled Donkey, Kwei-li ran to tell her mother where she and Shan were going. As they would probably reach the summer homes before their father, it was agreed that they should meet him at the gate of the first house.

"Be sure to meet your father," said their mother a bit anxiously, as Shan and Kwei-li set forth on their donkey.

Shan felt important as they rode along, because he knew the way and because he had charge of his own small basket. From time to time he lifted the cloth that covered the vegetables, and looked at the red carrots and curly cabbage leaves.

Kwei-li was not thinking about vegetables, but about another little girl on another donkey. Shan had said that the little girl lived beyond the rocky point, and maybe Kwei-li would see her today!

Kwei-li thought, I am just like that little girl, except that my donkey has no bells on his reins. She forgot that her jacket was faded, and that there was a patch on her trousers, and that the other little girl had been dressed in silk.

The tide was low, so Shan took the road along the beach, which he liked better than the shorter road through the fields. Riding Donkey, they were sure to reach the first house before Father did, and they could ride clear around the point when the tide was low.

"When we get to that point of rocks," Shan

told Kwei-li, "I will show you the pirate's cave!"

"What pirate's cave?" asked Kwei-li.

"A cave where pirates hid their treasure long ago," said Shan, who had been to the rocky point with other village boys.

Donkey trotted gaily. The load on his back seemed light to him. Trot, trot, went his hoofs on the wet, hard sand. The rocky point had seemed far off, but now the rocks loomed close, and they were larger than the rocks below Locust Village. They looked like a pile of stones that some giant had put on the sand. In one place two slanting rocks formed a deep cave.

"Look!" cried Shan, as they drew near. "There is the pirate's cave!"

"Where?" asked Kwei-li.

Shan pointed and, as he pointed, Donkey

gave a jump because of a starfish that lay in his
path. The jump dislodged the children, who
bounced off his back and landed, plump, with
the vegetables, right at the mouth of the cave.

"Ay-ah," cried Shan. "Don't let Donkey
run away!"

Kwei-li caught hold of the donkey's reins,
while Shan picked up the basket. The vegetables were scattered here and there among the
seaweed. Shan gathered them up as best he
could and popped them back in the basket.

"Father may get there first, after all, and he
will scold us," said Shan.

But Kwei-li was not worried about what her
father would say. Her eyes were searching the
depths of this cave she had never seen before.
"Stand still, Donkey," she said. For she saw
shells and shells, piled up in a glistening bank
within the cave.

While Shan tucked the rumpled cloth over the sandy vegetables, Kwei-li darted inside the cave to pick up a handful of shells. There was a double pink one, shaped like a butterfly, and a lavender one with a black band, also double.

"Shan, Shan," said Kwei-li. "Help me gather shells." She didn't want to hurry on and leave all the shells behind.

"We cannot stop and play," said Shan. "We must go on our way."

"Donkey will stand still," said Kwei-li. "Wait just a little while."

Shan was impatient. "Don't you want to sell vegetables?" he said. "Don't you want to take money home to Mother?"

"Here is money," said Kwei-li, stooping swiftly, for she had seen a flash of silver among the sea shells.

Shan's eyes widened. What was this his sister had found? It was something silver, and it looked like money. It was a silver bracelet, made of coins linked together, each carved with a delicate pattern.

"It is money," said Kwei-li.

"No," said Shan, "it is a silver bracelet. It is made to look like silver money, but it is only a bracelet. Probably," he added, "some pirate left it there."

"I can keep it then," said Kwei-li.

Shan nodded. "Yes, you can keep it."

Kwei-li had a pocket on the inside of her jacket, and she filled her pocket with a family of shells. But she fastened the pirate's silver bracelet around one wrist, where it fitted just as though it had been made for her.

Now the children were ready to continue their journey. Shan helped Kwei-li on Donkey's back and gave her the basket to hold.

Then he climbed up himself and slapped the donkey's reins. Off they went, and soon they had rounded the long point of rocks.

Here was another bay and here was another beach and, beyond the beach, on the firm land, was a row of houses. Each was set in its own low-walled garden, and Kwei-li could see the tiled roofs showing above small pine trees and mimosa trees in bloom.

In one of those houses lived the little girl Kwei-li had seen. In the stable of one of those houses lived the donkey with jingling bells. Kwei-li looked around eagerly, expecting to see them. But the first person she saw was her own father.

He was waiting at the gateway of the nearest house, and in his hand was a cloth bag filled with copper money. "I have sold all my vegetables, and they brought a good price," he said.

"Where have you been so long? You have kept me waiting."

Shan and Kwei-li told him about their adventure.

But their father hardly noticed the bracelet Kwei-li wore. Instead, he examined the vegetables. "Too bad," he said. "If you had taken my road you might not have had a fall."

Shan's basket of vegetables did not sell for a high price, for they were mixed up with seaweed and covered with sand. But his father let him keep the copper coins that were paid for them. "You will do better another time, when you are more careful," he said.

Shan's copper coins were strung on a cord, and they were like a giant's bracelet, Kwei-li thought. But her own bracelet, with its silver coins, was a pirate's bracelet. She turned her wrist this way and that, admiring it.

Although she did not catch a glimpse of the other little girl, Kwei-li felt very happy, riding home to Locust Village. She would have felt even happier if her donkey had jingling bells ringing in time to his hoofbeats as he trotted along the road.

Chapter Seven

THE PIRATE'S CAVE

DINNER was waiting for the family when they returned home—bowls of fluffy rice topped with curled bean sprouts. Four pairs of chopsticks lay on the table, one pair for each person. Kwei-li picked hers up eagerly, for she was very hungry.

Her mother said, "What is that on your wrist, Kwei-li? A beautiful silver bracelet! Who gave it to you?"

"Nobody gave it to me. I found it," said Kwei-li.

"She found it in the pirate's cave on the beach," explained Shan.

Their mother looked puzzled. She knew about the pirate's cave and, when she was a little girl, she had found shells there. But no pirates had come to these shores for more than a hundred years. "Let me see the bracelet," she said. "It looks new to me."

Kwei-li held out her hand to her mother, who examined the linked bracelet, just the right size for a little girl. "It is new," she said. "Some little girl must have lost it."

"Yes," agreed Kwei-li's father. "Kwei-li must take it back."

But Kwei-li did not know how to take the bracelet back, because she did not know what little girl it happened to belong to. It might belong to the little girl who had the donkey, but Kwei-li did not know which house she lived in.

Her eyes filled with tears. "I don't want the bracelet," she said, slipping it off her hand. "The person that it belongs to can come here and get it." When she had finished eating she went out of the house. She didn't want to look at the bracelet any more.

At the end of the street Great-grandmother sat dozing in her doorway, with a quilt over her knees which she sewed on between naps. Her eyes opened and she smiled when she saw Kwei-li coming toward her. "You haven't come to see me for a long time," she said.

Kwei-li seated herself on the step beside

Great-grandmother, who was old and wise and knew about everything. Kwei-li told about her trip with Shan, and the bracelet she had found, and how her father had told her that she must take it back.

Great-grandmother listened, and nodded thoughtfully. "Your father is right, Kwei-li," she said, "for the bracelet is not yours. Take it back where you found it. That's my advice. Whoever lost it will surely come back to the same place and find it."

Kwei-li's face brightened. That was just what she would do! Not today, for she was tired, but some time tomorrow. She forgot to tell Great-grandmother exactly where she had found the bracelet, and Great-grandmother did not know she would have to go so far.

The next morning Kwei-li went with Shan to the vegetable garden, where the three watermelon plants were growing vigorously. Small melons, striped with dark green and light green, lay hidden under the broad leaves. They were larger than hen's eggs and growing bigger every day.

While Shan was busy pulling up turnips, Kwei-li slipped away. She did not want Shan to go with her to the pirate's cave. He might tease her about the bracelet that she had to take back. No, Kwei-li thought, I can go by myself, because I know the way.

The journey along the beach seemed long today, without Donkey to carry her, but there was no danger of getting lost on the bare, flat sand. Kwei-li could go fast in her red shoes, which had no holes in the toes. They were not new any more, but one was newer than the other.

The tide was coming in, but Kwei-li did not

think about that. She did not even think about stopping to look for double shells. All she could think about was her errand and the bracelet in her pocket—the beautiful silver bracelet that did not belong to her.

The bracelet felt heavy, because she could not forget it. She would be happy, Kwei-li thought, when she laid it in the cave. Then she would run home, feeling light and free, knowing that the bracelet's owner would come and find it.

The rocks loomed up ahead of her, big and dark. Some were covered with moss, while others were worn smooth by the waves. Spray dashed against the farthest ones that jutted out into the sea. The tide was coming in fast, but Kwei-li did not know that.

She followed the narrowing beach until she came to the pirate's cave. Here it was, and here was the spot where Donkey had shied at a starfish. All at once Kwei-li wished that she had asked Shan to come with her, for the cave looked dark and awesome when she was all by herself.

She walked inside timidly. Everything was different today. The bright pile of shells was covered with tangled seaweed. The tide has been here, thought Kwei-li. It had come right up inside the cave since she and Shan had been here the day before.

The tide did strange things. It kept coming in, sometimes in the morning and sometimes at night. Sometimes it carried shells with it; sometimes it took them away. But what if the next tide should carry away the bracelet?

The little girl who owned the bracelet would come to look for it, and Kwei-li must not let the sea carry it away. As she searched about inside the cave for a high, safe place, she saw some rough ledges up above her head.

If Shan were here, he would be able to reach up and place the bracelet on a rough ledge of rock. Kwei-li could not reach so high and, besides, the other little girl—the one the bracelet belonged to—might not see it there.

The sand sloped upward toward the back of the cave and there, in a far corner, Kwei-li carefully laid the bracelet. She hoped the waves would not reach back here. She hoped it would be safe. With her errand over, she hurried back to the entrance of the cave.

But Kwei-li could not run home, light and free, for the sea was washing around the point and the beach was disappearing. She started toward home, but a great wave wet her shoes. She would have to take off her shoes and go barefooted.

Kwei-li took off her shoes and once more started for home, holding a precious shoe in each hand. Before she had gone very far a bigger wave rushed at her. It splashed up to her knees, and Kwei-li felt frightened. It was not really far to the higher, dryer sand that curved homeward from the point of rocks to Locust Village. But Kwei-li feared that another wave might come right over her head! Feeling still more frightened, she ran back to the cave.

Far back, where the bracelet lay, the sand was high and dry. The waves can't get me here, thought Kwei-li hopefully. She decided to wait there until the big waves turned into small ones, and she could put her shoes on and walk safely home.

Chapter Eight

HOW KWEI-LI WAS RESCUED

SHAN kept on working in the vegetable garden and, when he noticed that Kwei-li had left, he wasn't at all surprised. She had probably found a cricket and gone home, he thought. He never once thought about the bracelet, or the pirate's cave. But when Shan returned home he saw only his mother, and his father, who sat on the doorstep, mending a net.

"Where is Kwei-li?" said his mother. "It is time that she came home."

"It is going to rain," said his father, looking at the sky. "Why didn't Kwei-li come home with you, Shan?"

Shan told his father and mother that Kwei-li had left the garden. "Perhaps she is at Bluebell's house," he suggested.

But Kwei-li was not at Bluebell's house.

"I will go to Great-grandmother's house. She might be there," said Kwei-li's mother.

But Great-grandmother had not seen Kwei-li since the day before. "She told me about finding a bracelet," said Great-grandmother. "It belonged to somebody else, and I advised her to take it back. Perhaps she has gone to take it back and will return soon."

Kwei-li's mother was troubled. It was going to rain, and she did not know where her daughter could be. She did not think that Kwei-li would go to the pirate's cave by herself. But when she told Kwei-li's father what Great-grandmother had said, Shan pricked up his ears. "I know where Kwei-li is!" he cried. "She must have gone back to the cave!"

The silver bracelet was not in the house, and his father and mother agreed that Kwei-li might have taken it all the way back to the cave. But the cave was a dangerous place to be when the tide was coming in!

"I will saddle Donkey and ride after Kwei-li," said Shan eagerly.

His father said, "No, Shan. The tide is coming in fast. It is better for me to go after Kwei-li in my boat." He knew that by this time the waves were splashing around the rocky point, but he could row there in his boat and rescue Kwei-li.

"Hurry, hurry," said Kwei-li's mother. "Bring Kwei-li safely home!"

Rain had begun to fall when Kwei-li's father reached the beach where the fishing boats were lined up in a row. He started to push his boat down toward the water, wishing that he had stopped to ask someone else to go with him and help. And suddenly he felt that there *was* someone else. Shan was at his side, helping to push.

"Climb in the boat, Shan," said his father, when the boat was in the water. "We can bring Kwei-li safely home together!"

All this time Kwei-li was in the pirate's cave, waiting for the big waves to turn into small ones. But instead of getting smaller, they got bigger and bigger. The biggest ones came right up to the mouth of the cave.

When the sky became dark and rain pattered down, the inside of the cave grew nearly as black as night. Kwei-li did not care any longer for her far, dry corner. She ran to the cave opening and stared out at the sea. Her big straw hat was like an umbrella, so she didn't mind the rain that rolled down its brim. But she didn't like the waves that rolled toward her bare toes. She wished that someone, her father or Shan, would come to find her.

There was no fishing fleet on the horizon, where rain clouds had piled up so suddenly. The sea was dotted over with dancing raindrops, but they did not stop the tide from coming in and coming in.

Somewhere on that gray sea were her father and Shan, but it was not their boat that Kwei-li saw when finally she spied a boat. This boat was coming from the beach where the summer houses were, and there were two people in it, a man and a little girl. Kwei-li could not see their faces, but they were coming toward her. She took off her hat and waved it, so that they would be sure to see her.

"Come and get me!" she called.

The man in the boat turned his head. "I hear someone calling," he said.

"I see someone!" cried the little girl. "Look! In front of the cave!"

"I see a little girl with a big straw hat," said the man. "She must have got caught in the cave when the tide was coming in."

The little girl in the boat peered anxiously from under a great umbrella that was coated with oil so that rain could not soak through it. She thought she had seen Kwei-li before, but

she wasn't sure. "Hurry, Father," she said. "She is getting wet!"

Her father smiled at his daughter, whose name was Jewel, and pulled harder on the oars. Since he was not used to rowing, he had not wanted to bring her out in a boat in the rain, but she had begged so hard that he couldn't refuse. Neither he nor Jewel had expected to find a little girl when they set forth to look for a lost bracelet. Jewel had lost it the day before while gathering sea shells in the cave, and they thought it might be there still if the tide had not carried it away.

Kwei-li did not recognize Jewel at first, but she was happy, because the boat was coming toward the cave. Someone must have known just where she was! And whoever the people in the boat were, she was sure they were friends of hers.

As the boat drew nearer and nearer she grew even happier, for here was the same little girl who had ridden by on a donkey! Suddenly Kwei-li thought of the bracelet. It must be this little girl's bracelet. She ran back into the cave to get it, so that she could give it to her.

Kwei-li's hat was heavy with rain. She dropped it on the sand beside the shoes that she had not wanted to get wet. Here was the bracelet, right where she had left it! She ran back excitedly, clasping it in her hand.

Jewel's father had rowed the boat close to the mouth of the cave, but he did not need to get out to look for his daughter's lost treasure. For there it was, shining in Kwei-li's outstretched hand.

"Oh," cried Jewel, "the little girl has found my bracelet!"

She was glad to see her bracelet again, but

gladder still to rescue Kwei-li, who was soaked
with rain from her head to her toes. While
her father steadied the boat with his oars, Jewel
reached out her umbrella and said, "Catch hold
of the umbrella and climb into our boat."

"We will take you home," added her father,
holding out one hand.

Kwei-li was already so wet that she didn't
mind getting wetter. She waded out into the
water, holding out her arms. Then, with the
help of Jewel's umbrella and Jewel's father's
hand, she scrambled up into the boat and sat
beside Jewel.

Now Kwei-li was able to give the bracelet
back to its owner. She was glad that the owner
had turned out to be Jewel. She was glad that,
like her own father, Jewel's father had a boat
and could row her safely home from the pirate's
cave.

The tide did not have a chance to carry away the bracelet, and the waves did not have a chance to roll over Kwei-li. Kwei-li and Jewel sat side by side under the big umbrella, and Jewel's father rowed them away through the falling rain.

The water was as high as it would get on this tide, and in a few moments the waves would be getting smaller and smaller. But Shan and his father were filled with dismay when they reached the cave and Kwei-li was nowhere to be seen. All they could find, just above the high-water mark, was Kwei-li's hat, lying where she had dropped it. Close beside it was a pair of red cloth shoes—Kwei-li's shoes, which she had forgotten.

Chapter Nine

THE BEAUTIFUL HOUSE

THERE was excitement in Locust Village, for Shan and his father had returned home without finding Kwei-li. She might have waded around the rocks, they said hopefully. But she had not found her way home through the millet fields.

Her mother gazed sorrowfully at Kwei-li's hat and shoes, all that had been brought back from the pirate's cave. "Ay-ah," she cried, "Kwei-li is lost!" She dared not think that the dangerous tide had caught Kwei-li.

Everyone in the village who was able was going to search for Kwei-li. Bluebell took her little brother by the hand and went to look in the fields. Li and Lan, with some other boys, went to look on the beach. They clambered over every rock and peered into every deep crack.

Kwei-li's father and the other men scattered over the countryside, some riding mules or donkeys, and some on foot. But Kwei-li's mother stayed at home, waiting for Kwei-li, and Great-grandmother, who was too old to walk far, came to comfort her.

Shan was busy saddling Donkey when he

heard Great-grandmother say, "Kwei-li will come back. You wait and see."

But Shan was not going to wait! He was going to ride on the swift donkey to where he thought Kwei-li might be.

When Jewel's father said to Kwei-li, "We will take you home," Kwei-li thought that of course he would take her to her own home. She never guessed that he was taking her to Jewel's home, until he rowed around the point straight toward the summer houses.

"There is our house," said Jewel, pointing to the largest one.

"That is not my house," said Kwei-li.

"No, it is mine," said Jewel. "We are going there, and you can stay and play with me until it stops raining."

She glanced at her father as she spoke.

Her father nodded. "Yes, you may play with this little girl for a while," he said. "What is your name, and where do you live?" he asked Kwei-li.

"I am Kwei-li, and I live in Locust Village," said Kwei-li.

"Ah, yes," said Jewel's father. "That is not very far away."

But the village seemed far away to Kwei-li as she followed Jewel through the gateway of her house. Kwei-li wanted to turn and run home, but the rain was still falling, and Jewel's hand held hers.

"Come," said Jewel.

Jewel had many toys and several pets, but she had no little girl of her own age to play with. She wanted to show all her toys to her new friend. She wanted to be very kind to the little girl she had rescued.

She led Kwei-li, who held back timidly, into the beautiful house where her mother sat at a carved table, arranging flowers in a vase. Kwei-li remembered to bow, as she had been taught to do.

"Who is this little girl?" asked Jewel's mother, smiling.

Jewel told how she and her father had found Kwei-li, and how Kwei-li in turn had found her bracelet. "See," she said, holding out her hand to her mother.

Jewel's mother was happy to see the lost bracelet, but her eyes turned quickly back to Kwei-li's small, wet figure. "I think you should give your little friend some dry clothes," she told Jewel. "When the rain stops we must send her home to her family."

But Jewel didn't want to send Kwei-li home. "Let her stay and play with me all day," she begged. "I want to show her all my toys, and my pets, and my garden!"

Jewel's mother, like her father, found it very hard to say no to her only daughter. "Find her some dry clothes and let her play for a while," she said. Later, Jewel's father could take her home himself.

Kwei-li had never before seen a house with such large, airy rooms, all with cool matting on the floor, and with glass-paned windows. She had never seen such pretty clothes as the ones Jewel took from a chest in her room and spread out before her, for her to put on. There were green trousers, a pink jacket, purple embroidered shoes. Shoes! Kwei-li suddenly remembered that she had left her own shoes behind.

Her eyes grew wide with distress. "I must go back for my shoes," she said.

"You cannot go back for your shoes," said Jewel. "Look, I will give you mine."

But Kwei-li did not want to put on Jewel's pretty shoes. They were too big for her, and they were not hers. Tears rolled down her cheeks as she let Jewel help her put on dry clothes, but she would not slip the shoes on her feet, "I want to go home," she said.

Jewel felt distressed too. "Stay with me," she begged. "You can go home later. My father will take you. I will let you play with all my toys."

So Kwei-li stopped crying and looked at Jewel's toys, though she would not play with them. There were dolls, a whole family of beautiful dolls. There were tops, big and small ones, and there was a tiny sewing box. There was a doll's tea set and there were clay animals —a monkey, a tiger, and a row of little cats.

Then Jewel showed Kwei-li her pet canary, which sang sweetly from its perch in a fancy bamboo cage.

Kwei-li thought at once of her own bird made of paper. "I have a bird too," she said.

"Does it sing?" asked Jewel.

Kwei-li did not answer, so Jewel took her hand and led her out into the garden, for it had stopped raining. "Here are all my flowers. You may pick some if you like," she said.

Kwei-li stood still for a moment, looking at the flowers. There were asters, and lilies, and peonies growing in pots, and they were all beaded with raindrops and shining like jewels.

But Kwei-li could not see any vegetables in the garden, and she thought of her carrots and turnips and round green melons. "I have a garden, too," she said to Jewel. "And I have watermelons growing in my garden!"

Jewel looked disappointed. She didn't have any watermelons. "Well, come and see my donkey," she said at last.

Kwei-li followed Jewel into the kitchen courtyard. There in a stable, munching hay, stood a plump donkey. Its back was smooth and gray, its legs were long, and it looked almost exactly like Kwei-li's donkey. But there was one difference: around its neck were woven reins, hung with jingling bells. Kwei-li stared at them wistfully.

"You haven't any donkey, have you?" said Jewel.

"Oh yes, I have a donkey!" said Kwei-li. Of course she had one.

Jewel looked astonished. Couldn't she show this little girl anything at all that she did not have?

Yes, there was one thing—the donkey bells.

"My donkey hasn't any bells to wear," said Kwei-li softly.

Jewel's face brightened. "Never mind," she said. "You have no bells for your donkey, but *I* haven't any watermelons!"

The two little girls smiled at each other, for each one had something the other did not have. And they might have played together all the afternoon, like old friends, if something hadn't happened just then. A donkey brayed beyond the courtyard wall, and its braying was answered by Jewel's donkey.

"Listen to my donkey," exclaimed Jewel.

"It sounds like *my* donkey!" cried Kwei-li.

Then, above the sound of the donkeys' braying, they heard a knock, knocking at the courtyard gate. It was Shan knocking! When the gate was opened, there he stood, holding Donkey's bridle.

"I guessed you were here," said Shan proudly. "I guessed because of the silver bracelet." He had ridden straight to the summer houses and knocked at each gate until he found the right one.

As Kwei-li rode home through the fields with Shan, she felt very happy and she looked very gay. Jewel had told her she must keep the new clothes she wore. That was because Kwei-li had found the bracelet.

The pink jacket was pretty and so were the green trousers, but Kwei-li was anxious to put on her own shoes. She was glad when Shan told her that he had brought them home.

"I will never lose them again," promised Kwei-li.

When she was at home, safe and sound, the people of Locust Village came flocking to Kwei-li's house to make sure she was back.

"We looked for you everywhere," said Li.

"We thought you were lost, or drowned," said Lan.

"But I knew that Shan would find you," said Great-grandmother.

Kwei-li's mother could hardly believe that this was her own daughter, dressed so finely in silken clothes. She smiled as Kwei-li told her about the visit with Jewel, and about the kindness of the rich people who had rescued her.

"Tell me about the house," she said. "Was it very beautiful?"

"It was bigger than ours," said Kwei-li. And that was all she would say.

Chapter Ten

TWO GIFTS

THERE were only three watermelon vines in the vegetable garden, but the melons upon these vines grew extra big. Kwei-li's father was proud of them, for they were fine and juicy, dark green on the outside, bright red within.

The first one that ripened on the vine he

brought home to his family. "Look at this!" he cried, cutting it open with a knife. "Did you ever see such a beautiful melon? Just taste it!"

Kwei-li tasted her portion, which was as sweet as honey.

But Jewel, who was her friend, didn't have any watermelons, so Kwei-li asked her father if she might give her one.

"Jewel's father will pay a good price for it," put in Shan.

But Kwei-li had not meant that, at all. The melon must be a gift!

Kwei-li's father and mother agreed. The melon should be a gift. So the very next melon that ripened was carried to Jewel's house. There it was cut open and eaten by Jewel and her family, who declared it was the best watermelon that they had ever tasted.

It was not long afterwards that Kwei-li received a gift, a parting present from Jewel, who was leaving for the city. Kwei-li was delighted when she saw what it was—woven reins hung with jingling bells to put around Donkey's neck!

Kwei-li was sorry for her friend, who had to go back to the city, leaving her beautiful summer house empty and cold. Her own house, with its two rooms, would stay snug and warm all winter long, no matter how many winds blew.

When the summer was over, Kwei-li and Shan did not care to play on the beach, and it was a long, long time before they ventured again to the pirate's cave. But they rode their donkey every day, and the sound of the jingling bells could be heard through Locust Village and all over the countryside.

In the spring Shan would be old enough to go out with the fishing fleet and help his father and the other men pull in their great net. And Kwei-li would be old enough to polish the best teakettle and help her mother wash the rice bowls and set them in a row.